P9-DGG-083

PACHO NACHO

written by Silvia López

illustrated by Pablo Pino

CAPSTONE EDITIONS
a capstone imprint

Pacho Nacho is published by Capstone Editions,
a Capstone imprint
1710 Roe Crest Drive
North Mankato, Minnesota 56003
www.capstonepub.com

Library of Congress Cataloging-in-Publication Data
is available on the Library of Congress website.

ISBN 978-1-68446-098-4

Summary: When Pacho Nacho finds himself in trouble, his younger brother,
Juan, must quickly find help. But nothing seems quick when you have to
first say the name Pacho-Nacho-Nico-Tico-Melo-Felo-Kiko-Rico.

Designer: Hilary Wacholz

Printed in China.
2490

For my granddaughters, Leah and Katherine Morse—S.L.

Long ago in a little town in Mexico, Mamá and Papá cooed and fussed over their first baby boy. Papá loved the name Pacho. Mamá loved the name Nacho. They could not agree.

"Let's ask la familia!" Papá said.

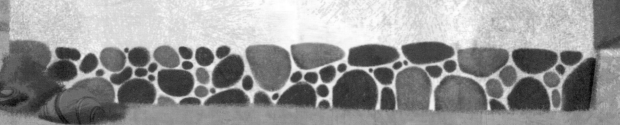

Los abuelos liked Nico. Las abuelas loved Tico. Los tíos proposed Melo. Las tías loved Felo. Los primos offered Kiko. Las primas loved Rico. No one could agree. Mamá and Papá wanted to please everyone, so they named him . . .

. . . Pacho-Nacho-Nico-Tico-Melo-Felo-Kiko-Rico.

A year later, Mamá and Papá cooed
and fussed over their second baby boy.
This time they couldn't think of a name.

"Let's ask la familia!" Mamá said.

But no one in the family could
think of a name either, so they
named him . . .

Mamá and Papá loved watching the boys grow.

They were proud of both boys, but they were especially proud of

Pacho-Nacho-Nico-Tico-Melo-Felo-Kiko-Rico's name.

"Always call your brother by his beautiful long name,"
they said over and over to Juan.

And los abuelos, las abuelas, los tíos, las tías, los primos,
and las primas made sure everyone in town did too.

As the boys got bigger and braver, they ventured farther and farther from home. Each day Mamá warned the boys about playing near the river.

"¡Cuidado! I don't want my precious darlings falling in!" she said. Then she would kiss the silky hair on top of their heads and send them off.

But even precious darlings with silky hair don't always mind their mothers. PaCHO–NaCHO–NiCO–TiCO–MELO–FELO–KiKO–RiCO and Juan were NOT careful at the river.

They chased croaking frogs.

They jumped on mossy rocks.

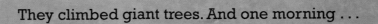

They climbed giant trees. And one morning . . .

Fast, fast, fast on his little feet Juan ran to his mother.
"¡Mamá! ¡Mamá!" he gasped. "Pacho Nacho is—"

"Mi amor," said Mamá. "Always call your brother by his beautiful long name."

Juan tried again. "Sí, sí, Mamá, but Pacho Nacho has—"

"Juan!" Mamá said firmly.

Juan took a deep breath.

"Pacho-Nacho-Nico-Tico-Melo-Felo-Kiko-Rico
may fall into the river!"

"¡Ay mi niño!" Mamá cried. "Get Papá!"

Fast, fast, fast on his little feet Juan ran to his father.
"¡Papá! ¡Papá!" he panted. "Pacho Nacho is—"

"Mi hijo," said Papá. "Always call your brother by his beautiful long name."

Juan tried not to cry. "Sí, sí, Papá, but Pacho Nacho has—"

"Juan!" Papá said sternly.

Juan took another deep breath.

"PACHO-NACHO-NICO-TICO-MELO-FELO-KIKO-RICO
may fall into the river!"

"¿Cómo?" exclaimed Papá. "Quick! To the boat!"

But then he stopped in his tracks. No oars! The old carpenter
was fixing them.

"Go get the oars, Juan!" Papá yelled. "¡Rápido!"

Fast, fast, fast on his little feet Juan ran to the old carpenter.
"Señor, señor," he wheezed. "Pacho Nacho is—"

"Muchacho," said the old carpenter. "Always call
your brother by his beautiful long name."

"Sí, sí, señor, but Pacho Nacho has—"

"Juan!" the carpenter said severely.

Juan rubbed his face. He huffed and puffed. He blew out his cheeks. Then he yelled at the top of his lungs:

"Pacho-Nacho-Nico-Tico-Melo-Felo-Kiko-Rico may fall into the river!"

"¡Caramba!" exclaimed the carpenter. "Why didn't you say so before?"

Fast, fast, fast on his old feet the carpenter brought Papá the oars.

With great urgency, Papá and the carpenter rowed and plucked the frightened Pacho–Nacho–Nico–Tico–Melo–Felo–Kiko–Rico from the broken branch.

Once on the shore, Mamá jiggled him. Papá wiggled him. And Juan tickled him until PACHO-NACHO-NICO-TICO-MELO-FELO-KIKO-RICO giggled.

"¡Ay, ay, ay!" Mamá sobbed. "To think one of our precious darlings could have fallen into the river!"

"All because of that long, silly name!" sniffled Papá. "Whatever should we do?"

Juan rolled his eyes. "Why not just call him PACHO NACHO?"

Mamá and Papá looked at each other and smiled. Mamá drew her boys close, and Papá beamed at Juan.

"¡Claro! What a smart boy!" he said, joining in the hug.

From that day on, Mamá and Papá forgot all about long, silly names. They called their boys Pacho Nacho and Juan.

And los abuelos, las abuelas, los tíos, las tías, los primos, and las primas made sure everyone else in town did too.

SPANISH WORDS

ay—oh

¡Ay mi niño!—Oh my boy!

¡Caramba!—Wow!

¡Claro!—Of course!

¿Cómo?—What?

¡Cuidado!—Careful!

la familia—the family

las abuelas—the grandmothers

las primas—the girl cousins

las tías—the aunts

los abuelos—the grandfathers

los primos—the boy cousins

los tíos—the uncles

mamá—mother

mi amor—my love

mi hijo—my son

muchacho—young man

papá—father

rápido—quickly

señor—sir

sí—yes

AUTHOR'S NOTE

The story of the boy with an extremely long name has been told as a folktale in Japan for hundreds of years. In that tale, the boy's name is *Jugemu jugemu, goko no surikire, kaijari suigyo no suigyomatsu, unraimatsu, furaimatsu, ku neru tokoro ni sumu tokoro, yabura koji no bura koji, paipo paipo, paipo no shuringan, shuringan no gurindai, gurindai no ponpokopi no ponpokona no, chokyumei no chosuke.*

Jugemu's story is still popular with Japanese children who dare each other to chant the name fast and without mistakes.

In 1924, Jugemu's tale was published in Great Britain in a book of children's stories. The setting was changed to China. The name also changed to *Tiki-tiki-tembo-no sa rembo-Hari bari broohski-Peri pen do-Hiki pon pom-Nichi no miano-Do.*

A later version did away with the Asian settings. Now set on a farm, the boy's name became *Eddie Cucha Catcha Camma Eddie Cucha Catcha Camma Toe-sa Nara Toe-sa Nocka Samma Camma Wacky Brown.* Eddie's story was so popular it was recorded by a singing group called The Brothers Four in 1960.

A few more versions followed until 1968, when the book *Tikki-Tikki-Tembo* was published by Arlene Mosel and illustrator Blair Lent. With the setting back in China, the story of the boy with the long name won several awards.

Years ago I realized that this old tale had found its way around three continents but had missed the Hispanic Americas altogether. I began writing my own version as a funny, repetition-filled story with a sprinkling of simple Spanish words. Pacho Nacho's full name is a string of popular Spanish boys' nicknames.

CREATORS

Silvia López learned to speak English when she was 10 years old. She is a Cuban native raised in Miami and served as children's librarian at schools and public libraries for more than three decades. She has written multiple picture books, including *Just Right Family: An Adoption Story, Handimals: Animals in Art and Nature*, and *Selena Quintanilla: Queen of Tejano Music*. López likes to write all types of stories in both English and Spanish. She wants to learn French as well, so look out!

Pablo Pino was born in Buenos Aires, Argentina, and grew up watching cartoons, playing football, and drawing. These days, he doesn't watch as much TV and only plays football once a week, but he still has the joy of painting every day. Pino works as a professional illustrator for different print media but enjoys illustrating books for children and teens best. Pablo is self-taught, and his illustrations are mostly computer drawn. But he always adds textures with pencils, crayons, acrylics, and pretty much any material that lets him get messy like when he was a child.